Carousel to the Stars

Stuart Lowry

illustrated by

Andrea Eberbach

Guild Press of Indiana, Inc.

© 2000 by The Children's Museum of Indianapolis

All rights reserved. No part of this book may be reproduced in any form without express permission from the publisher. For further information, contact

GUILD PRESS OF INDIANA, INC.
435 Gradle Drive
Carmel, Indiana 46032
(317) 848-6421

ISBN 1-57860-081-2

LIBRARY OF CONGRESS CATALOG CARD NUMBER 00-103423

Dust jacket art by Andrea Eberbach
Text and layout design by Sheila G. Samson
Printed in China

In memory of Mildred S. Compton —
a leader whose vision gave a treasure of the past
to the children of the future.

'Round and 'round with the sound of the wind,
up and down and around once again.
Cheers and laughs echo as we spin
'round and 'round and 'round.

Mine is a horse that nods to her friends,
yours a tiger with a fierce, frozen grin.
Mom and Dad hug their long-necked giraffes,
all coming 'round once again.

Goats and reindeer have joined in the chase.
A young golden lion prances proudly in place.
Pretty ponies believe that they'll win the race
as the calliope whistles a tune.

The room seems a sea as we swoop past the ground,
bright colors twirl in my horse's jeweled crown.
I float through the air in a flowing queen's gown,
dancing through time with delight.

The ocean swells and welcomes me,
I dive my horse into waves of the sea,
swimming with dolphins who leap to be free,
with a warm ocean wind as my guide.

'Round and 'round with the breeze at my tail,
up and down on the spout of a whale,
through day and a night my steed and I sail,
churning blue wave tops to white.

A shooting star flashes her sparkling light —
I grab her bright tail and soar out of sight.
But I'm caught by the moon who winks at the night
as he puts me back onto my mare.

'Round and 'round, we slow with the drum,
my horse pricks her ears as I whisper, "We're done."
But I promise we'll rise again, just like the sun,
and warm all our dreams into life.

One last kiss as soft as a tear,
then off through the gate I must disappear.
A new little rider climbs up with a cheer,
ready for magical flight.

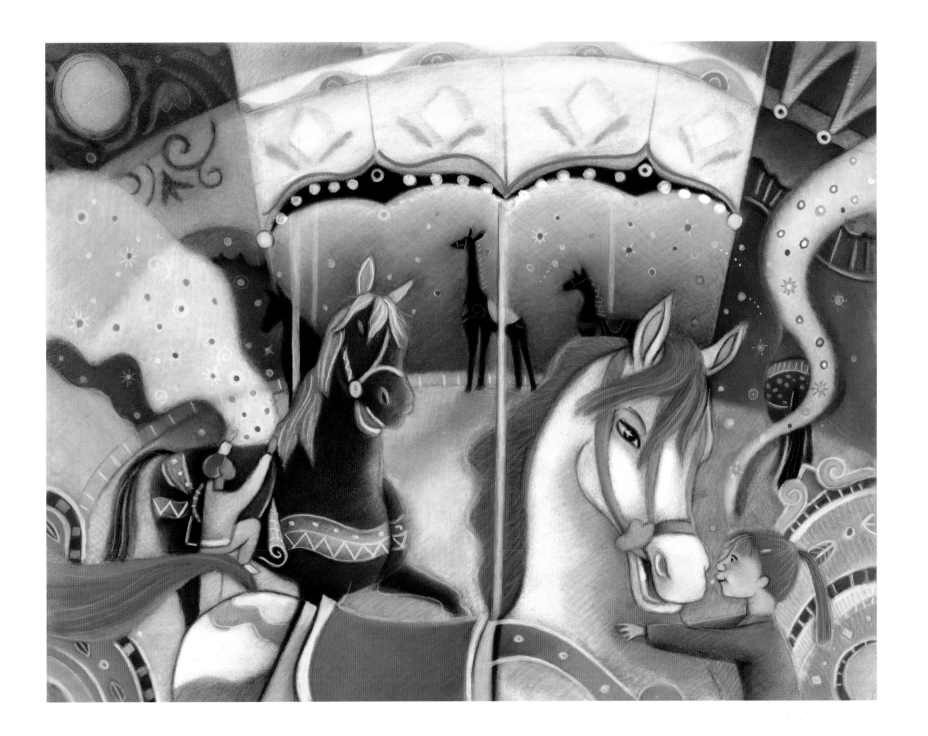

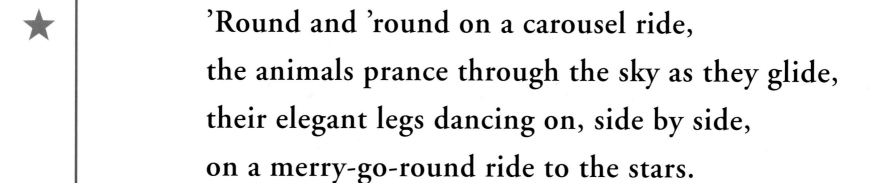

'Round and 'round on a carousel ride,
the animals prance through the sky as they glide,
their elegant legs dancing on, side by side,
on a merry-go-round ride to the stars.

The carousel in the Compton Gallery of The Children's Museum of Indianapolis (*above left*) became the shining attraction it is today through the efforts of skilled craftsmen who restored the animals and assembled the structure from pieces of old carousels (*center*), and through the dedication of Mildred Compton (*right*).

Carousels were first brought to America from Europe around the turn of the last century. The animals you see and that a child can ride today on the carousel at The Children's Museum of Indianapolis were carved about 1917 in Pennsylvania by Gustav Dentzel, a master carousel craftsman.

In their original carousel, these magnificent and fanciful animals offered rides to children in one of Indianapolis' most beautiful parks. Over time, it became apparent that the animals and calliope needed protection from the elements. Thus, in 1938, the carousel was moved under a large wooden dome in Broad Ripple Park. The dome sheltered the ride and the thousands of children who ultimately glided around on the carousel's majestic animals.

Time and weather took its toll on the dome, however, and it collapsed in 1956. No one was hurt in the incident, but the carousel was destroyed. The animals — although somewhat bruised, bumped, and scraped — survived. But they needed a new home and some loving care to restore them to their former glory. In the meantime, they were stored in a barn, with a few being brought out for special occasions, such as the big Christmas parade held in downtown Indianapolis each year.

Eventually, Mildred Compton, the director of The Children's Museum, heard of the plight of the old carousel animals. Recalling the warm, sunny days when she had taken her own children to ride the carousel at the park, Compton decided to rescue the animals for other children to love and enjoy.

Employing her talents for organization, Compton hired skilled craftsmen and artists to work on the animals. She and her staff also gathered enough carousel parts from all over America to recreate an authentic carousel. The restored ride and magnificent animals found their new home in The Children's Museum of Indianapolis. With a 1919 Wurlitzer organ to play lively, delightful tunes, the carousel was again ready to go 'round and 'round.

In 1976, the museum placed the carousel in its own special gallery on the top floor of the five-story building. There, the music and magic continue to invite visitors of all ages to take an enchanted ride.

After all, where better to dream and let one's imagination swirl to the stars than on the back of a magical beast at the top of the largest children's museum in the world?